Fairy School Drop-out

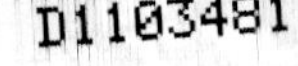

Fairy School Drop-out
this edition published in 2017 by
Hardie Grant Egmont
Ground Floor, Building 1, 658 Church Street
Richmond, Victoria 3121, Australia
www.hardiegrantegmont.com

The pages of this book are printed on paper derived from forests promoting sustainable management.

A CiP record for this title is available from the National Library of Australia

Cover design and illustration by Michelle Mackintosh
Text design by Sonia Dixon

Printed in China by Asia Pacific Offset

1 3 5 7 9 10 8 6 4 2

BY

MEREDITH BADGER

hardie grant EGMONT

Chapter one

If you happened to look through the kitchen window of 27 Raspberry Drive at 7.50 last Friday morning, you would have seen something so totally normal you wouldn't have thought twice about it. Mrs Knottleweed-Eversprightly was rushing around, trying to find her toolbox before she flew off to work. Mr Knottleweed-Eversprightly was there too, making sandwiches at the kitchen bench. Kara, the baby, was in her highchair, drooling as usual. And Kara's big sister Elly was eating her muesli and reading a comic book before she headed off for school. It was, in fact, all very dull. You might have even yawned a bit before you went on your way because the scene in the kitchen was so boring. Maybe you would've told yourself that you should really stop staring in other people's windows, because you never saw anything interesting anyway.

But if you had been a bit more patient and had stayed looking in the window a little longer, you would've seen something very strange start to happen. Not the sort of thing that happens in the average household at breakfast time at all. At 7.55, Elly's muesli bowl began to quiver. Two minutes later it started rocking from side to side. At exactly 8 o'clock, the muesli bowl hopped across the table seven times, splashing milk around as it did. Elly tried to pin it down with her spoon but the bowl kept sliding out of the way. Then at 8.01, the bowl floated up into the air.

'Stop that!' Elly said crossly, trying to grab it. 'Come back here immediately.'

But the muesli bowl continued floating higher and higher until it was positioned directly above her head. Elly had a feeling she knew what was coming next but there was nothing she could do except squeeze her eyes shut. Sure enough, the bowl tipped upside down and Elly found herself covered in sultanas and oats, with a river of cold milk flowing down the back of her neck.

Kara laughed and banged her spoon on her highchair. Elly removed a bran flake from her ear and glared at her baby sister.

'You did that on purpose,' she said. 'Everyone else might think you're cute and innocent but I know better. You're too smart for your own good.'

Kara did what any baby would do. She drooled some more. But this wasn't ordinary drool. Kara's drool sparkled like it was filled with tiny crystals.

Mrs Knottleweed-Everspightly rushed into the room.

'Elly, have you seen my …' she started, but stopped short when she saw her breakfast-covered daughter.

'What are you doing?' she asked crossly. 'There's no time for messing around. You

have to leave for school in a minute.'

'It wasn't me, Mum,' explained Elly. 'It was Kara.'

Mrs Knottleweed-Eversprightly shook her head sadly. 'Oh, Elly.'

Elly knew what her mum was thinking. 'But it's true!' she protested. 'Why won't anyone ever believe me that Kara knows magic? We're fairies after all, aren't we? We're supposed to do stuff like that.' It made Elly grumpy that no-one ever believed her. To make matters worse she could feel a cold, mushy bran flake sliding down her back.

Elly's mum sighed. 'Kara's far too young to know any magic.'

'Well, it wasn't me,' grumbled Elly, but there was no point arguing. The most annoying part was that Elly knew there was

no way she could've made the bowl rise like that, even though she was much older than Kara and was already going to one of the best fairy schools in Fairydom. In fact, Elly had already been to *three* of the best fairy schools in Fairydom – but unfortunately, she'd also been expelled from two of them. Both times it had been because of things she'd done accidentally, although no-one believed her. That was the problem with coming from a famous fairy family – everyone assumed that you knew exactly what you were doing when it came to magic.

Elly was prepared to admit that the first time she was thrown out of school was because of something silly she did. The drinking fountain in the toilets at Dandelion Grove School was broken so Elly had jammed

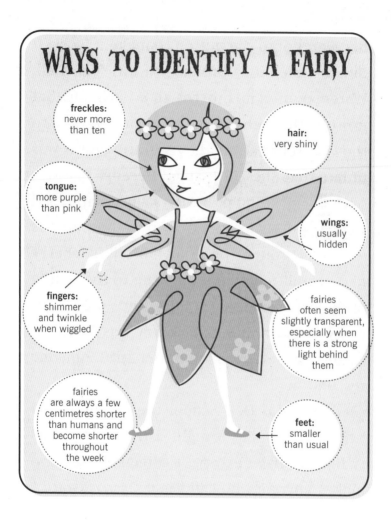

WAYS TO IDENTIFY A FAIRY

freckles: never more than ten

hair: very shiny

tongue: more purple than pink

wings: usually hidden

fingers: shimmer and twinkle when wiggled

fairies often seem slightly transparent, especially when there is a strong light behind them

fairies are always a few centimetres shorter than humans and become shorter throughout the week

feet: smaller than usual

her wand onto the button to make it work. It did the trick, but probably a little too well. Water spouted up into the air so strongly that it broke through the roof and surged up into the classroom above. Elly still thought it was unfair that she got blamed because she was only trying to help. But a teacher happened to be standing exactly on top of the water as it burst through the floor. Miss Pinkleberry had been lifted by the water up to the ceiling of the classroom. A wet fairy finds it difficult to fly so poor Miss Pinkleberry was forced to bounce up and down on the jet until someone rescued her.

At Crystal Dell School the problem had been because Elly caught a flyrus. A flyrus is like a virus, except it affects wings and makes anyone who catches it fly backwards.

Unfortunately, they are highly contagious and before long the whole school, including the teachers, were all flying backwards and bumping into each other. Elly was sent home to recover but when she was well again the Head Fairy suggested it might be best if Elly found another school. Elly thought this was mean. She hadn't *meant* to catch the flyrus after all.

Now she was at her third school – The Mossy Blossom Academy for Young Fairies. It had taken lots of effort by her parents to convince the school to take her. Madame Silverwings, the Head Fairy, had already been warned about Elly.

'This is your last chance,' her mother warned Elly on her first day. 'No other school will accept you if you're thrown out again and then you'll never get your Fairy Licence.'

Elly promised to try hard. And she *was* trying. It was just that things didn't always go the way she planned.

'Get changed, Elly,' said her mum as Elly trudged upstairs. 'And don't forget your wand!' she called after her.

Uh-oh ... Elly scrambled around in a pile of clothes until she found her wand. There was a great big dint in the handle. Elly gave it a shake and turned it on. The wand played its usual start-up tune but it sounded a little wonky. The star at the top was dim, too. Elly shook it again and the wand made a sound like a kitten whose tail had been stepped on. Great. The last thing Elly needed was a wand breakdown on top of everything else.

'Elly! It's time to leave!' called out Mrs Knottleweed-Everspightly.

Elly quickly tried to brush the muesli out of her hair and pulled on a clean school uniform. In the first year at Mossy Blossom, you had to wear a knee-length, baby-blue tutu. There was also a wreath of flowers for your head and soft blue slippers with big blue bows for your feet. Elly hated the uniform. She hated the itchy tutu and she hated the scratchy wreath. But most of all she hated the stupid shoes with those dumb, floppy bows. Elly's slippers were now splattered with milk. She took them off and pulled on her favourite red boots instead. Much better!

Her mum called again, impatiently. 'Come ON, Elly!'

Elly grabbed her skateboard and shoved it in her bag before dashing downstairs. Her mum caught her for a quick hug and a wet

kiss as she rushed out the door.

'Be good,' she said.

'Of course!' Elly replied, hoping her mum wouldn't look at her feet.

'And fly with the Fairy Flock this morning, OK?' called Mrs Knottleweed-Eversprightly as Elly dashed off. 'It'd be nice to have one week where your Head Fairy didn't call me up about some rule you've broken!'

'See you later!' called Elly over her shoulder. Maybe she could pretend she hadn't heard that last bit ...

Chapter two

Now, maybe you're reading this and thinking that Elly and her family don't sound like real fairies. Perhaps you think you're an expert because you've read all the fairy books and seen all the fairy movies. Well, forget all that stuff, because it's probably wrong. Most humans wouldn't recognise a fairy, even if there were one living right next door to them. And there might well be. For some reason, most humans think that fairies live in toadstools. Let's get one thing straight right from the start. *They don't*. They live in houses, just like humans. Don't believe it? Have a look at the size difference between a fairy and a toadstool:

Would *you* want to live in a toadstool? Exactly. Neither would a fairy.

Here are some other lesser-known fairy facts:

1. Although fairies are naturally very small (about the size of a ten-year-old's hand) they can stretch themselves up to human proportions using an Anatomical Resizing Machine. They have to do this every week, however, because fairies soon start shrinking back to their normal size.

2. Humans often live in the same streets as fairies without realising. This is just the way fairies like it. Imagine if humans knew that they had fairies living next door – they would be constantly hassling them to grant wishes and fix things. Fairies prefer to choose for themselves *whose* wishes – and *which* wishes – they grant.

3. Most fairies aren't born knowing magic. They learn it at school. Then after three years' study, they receive their Fairy Licence which qualifies them to do spells.

4. To avoid being recognised, fairies keep their wings tucked away under their clothes or hidden in special wing-hiding backpacks. Sometimes, if you look carefully, you can see the slots in their clothes where the wings usually pop through.

5. There are boy fairies as well as girl fairies. Boy fairies can't fly or do magic but they are often excellent cooks.

And here's a fairy fact
that might really
surprise you:

6. Not all fairies like being fairies.

Elly was one such fairy. She didn't just *not like* being a fairy, she *hated* it. She hated it more than paper cuts. More than cold baths. More than jam and anchovy sandwiches. What exactly did she hate about it? Everything. The stuff she was meant to wear. The things she was meant to learn. But most of all, she hated flying. Flying might look like fun but Elly found it tiring and boring. Besides, skateboarding was so much more fun.

Elly had spent a lot of time working on her skateboard. She only had the standard fairy model – the Star Grazer I – but it was even faster than a Star Grazer III because of all the extra work she'd done on it. She'd saved up for rainbow speed wheels that spun so fast they left a rainbow pattern behind them on the path. As a finishing touch, Elly

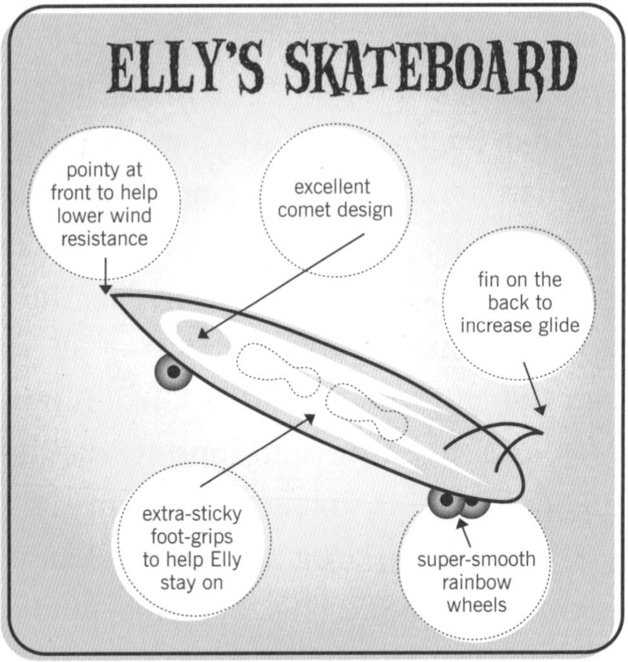

ELLY'S SKATEBOARD

pointy at front to help lower wind resistance

excellent comet design

fin on the back to increase glide

extra-sticky foot-grips to help Elly stay on

super-smooth rainbow wheels

had painted a cool silver comet across the board. Skateboarding was definitely Elly's favourite way to get around.

So the moment she got around the corner from her house Elly got her skateboard out of her bag. She was just about to ride off when she remembered what her mother had said about catching the Fairy Flock to school.

The Fairy Flock was another thing Elly hated about being a fairy. It was the way most fairies got to school, travelling in one big group disguised as a cloud. The passengers had to wear cloud coats – floaty, white garments that looked like they were made from cotton-wool, with slots in the back for wings to stick through. As the flock passed overhead, fairies waiting on the ground flew up to join it. From a distance the Fairy Flock looked just like a soft white cloud, drifting across the sky. Most humans wouldn't think twice about it. But then most humans aren't very observant. If they paid more attention they would notice that some clouds travel very rapidly across the sky. If they listened more carefully they might even hear voices seemingly coming from nowhere, saying things like 'Ow! Stop pushing!' and 'Wait ... this is my stop!'

Elly couldn't decide what to do. She knew she should do what her mum said, but catching the flock was terrible. As she stood there deciding, she heard a voice behind her. Not a very pleasant voice.

'Well, if it isn't the fairy school drop-out,' it said. 'Thinking about travelling the *normal* way today, are you?'

Without even looking Elly knew who it was. Gabilotta Cruddleperry, also known as Gabi. Gabi was Mossy Blossom's star pupil and one look at her explained why. Her hair was perfect, her cloud-coat was perfect and her neatly packed bag was undoubtedly filled with perfect homework. For some reason, Gabi had taken a dislike to Elly right from the first day of school. This might've been because Elly had accidentally made Gabi grow a big bushy moustache during their first Spelling lesson. Elly had apologised, of course, and had removed the moustache (which curled up magnificently at the ends) the moment she worked out how. But things were never the same after that.

Seeing Gabi helped Elly make up her mind.

'Actually,' said Elly, putting her skateboard on the ground again, 'I'm going to ride.'

Gabi frowned. 'It's against the Fairy Code, you know.'

'Oh yeah?' said Elly. 'Where does it say that?'

'Page 539, paragraph two,' replied Gabi.

ELLY'S FAMILY TREE

Great-great-great-great-grandmother:
Mattina Knottleweed-Eversprightly. Co-author of the Fairy Code and several other books on wing management, elegant flying and correct wand grip.

Great-great-great-grandmother:
Katyana Knottleweed-Eversprightly.
A Head Fairy who campaigned for longer school days and more difficult exams.

Great-great-grandmother:
Hilaretta Knottleweed-Eversprightly. A famous fairy athlete, who held the air-speed record for twenty years.

Great-grandmother:
Triciella Knottleweed-Eversprightly.
An explorer who travelled extensively throughout the human world, disguised as a gypsy.

Grandmother:
Fifibella Knottleweed-Eversprightly.
A well-known author and journalist.

Mother:
Julerina Knottleweed-Eversprightly.
A Fairydom-renowned inventor who works for the famous Fairy Inc Corporation.

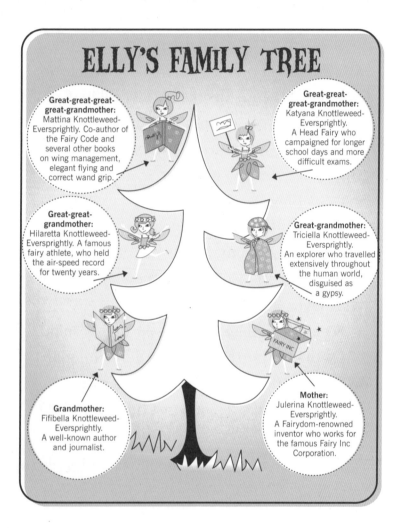

‘It says: *The only way in which a school fairy should travel to and from school is by flying or walking*. You should know that. After all, wasn’t it one of your ancestors who wrote the Fairy Code in the first place?’

Elly shrugged. ‘Maybe.’ It was hard to keep track of her family’s achievements sometimes. They’d all done so much.

A puffy white cloud appeared on the horizon, moving fast. The Fairy Flock. It looked like a particularly wriggly, squirmy cloud today. Elly jumped on her skateboard.

‘Don’t get your wings scrunched!’ Elly called to Gabi as she zoomed down the street. She didn’t have to turn around to know that Gabi was watching her leave, shaking her head in disapproval.

Chapter three

When Elly arrived at school, her friend Sapphire was waiting for her. Sapphire was the perfect name for her because she had the biggest, bluest eyes you could ever see. Elly sometimes teased her that she looked like the sort of fairy humans drew pictures of. Saphie was just as smart as Gabi but was much, much nicer.

'Hi, Saphie!' said Elly, quickly shoving her skateboard in her bag.

'Hi!' said Saphie. 'Did you get my wand-message? I sent one last night reminding you about this morning's spelling test.'

Elly fished out her wand, which was looking worse than ever. There were even some bite marks from where Kara had been chewing on it. Elly clicked a button and the wand whined unhappily. Finally, after a lot of spluttering, Saphie's face appeared in the centre of the star. She was urgently mouthing words but no sound was coming out.

'I think it's broken,' explained Elly, as Saphie's wand-message dissolved into static. She shook the wand again and it made a sloshing noise.

'I must have dropped it in the bath,' Elly frowned.

Saphie took the wand and checked how

much power it had. It was almost empty. She looked at her friend and raised an eyebrow.

'It'd probably help if you remembered to charge it up occasionally,' she grinned.

'Yes,' agreed Elly ruefully. 'That's true.'

Before starting fairy school, Elly had thought it would be cool to have a wand, but that was back when she thought all you needed to do was wave one around and say a few weird words for the magic to work. It turned out that wands were much more complicated than that. It took lots of practice to make them work properly. They came with manuals that were almost as thick as the wands were high, and were about as easy to read as flying backwards through a hailstorm. Elly had lost her manual ages ago anyway, and ever since then she'd just been guessing how to use it. Guessing incorrectly most of the time, as it turned out.

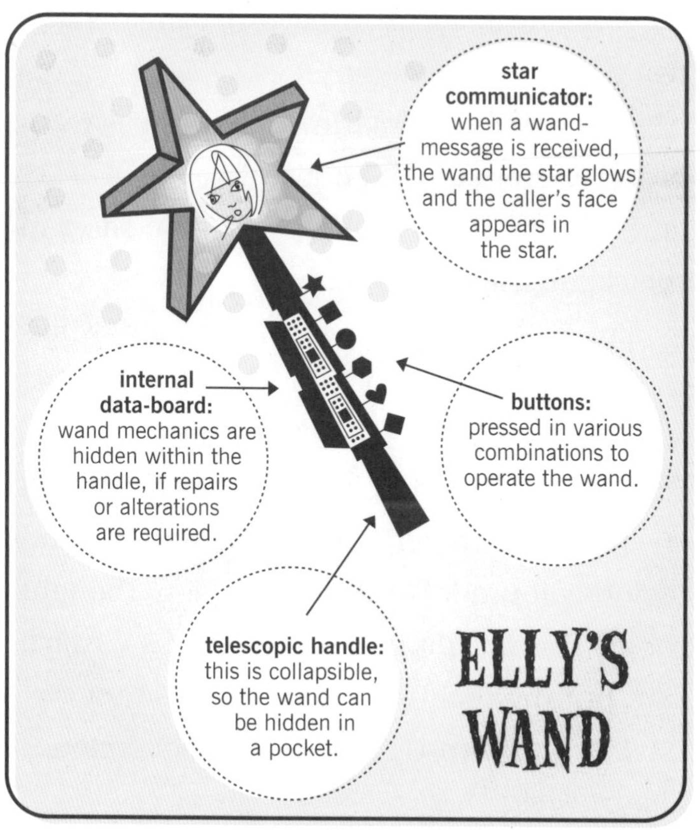
star
communicator:
when a wand-
message is received,
the wand the star glows
and the caller's face
appears in
the star.
internal
data-board:
wand mechanics are
hidden within the
handle, if repairs
or alterations
are required.
buttons:
pressed in various
combinations to
operate the wand.
telescopic handle:
this is collapsible,
so the wand can
be hidden in
a pocket.
ELLY'S
WAND

Saphie tugged Elly's arm. 'Come on,' said Saphie. 'We have to hurry. You know Mrs Clovercloud likes us to be early on spelling-test days.'

Elly snorted. 'Mrs Clovercloud likes us to be early *every* day. She also likes us to stay late. In fact, if she had her way we'd sleep in the classroom overnight.'

But Saphie was already in the air, wings fluttering.

'Come on,' she urged. 'Let's go.'

The two girls flew around the corner and straight into something warm, squishy and lemon-coloured. For a moment, Elly thought they'd flown right into an enormous custard tart, but the reality was far less pleasant.

They'd flown right into Mrs Clovercloud. She frowned.

'Fairies! What does the Fairy Code say about flying around corners?'

Elly sighed. The Fairy Code was the first book fairies received when they started school. It was three times as thick as the wand manual and, as far as Elly was concerned, even less interesting to read. It described how fairies were expected to behave and what to do in emergencies. By the end of three years at school, all fairies were supposed to know the code back-to-front. It was even worse for Elly because some ancient relative of hers was supposedly one of the original authors, and so everyone thought that she already knew it back-to-front.

She didn't.

Luckily for Elly, Saphie knew the answer to Mrs Clovercloud's question.

'Fairies must approach a corner at the lowest possible speed and should sound a warning with their wand,' she recited.

Mrs Clovercloud nodded. 'Remember that next time, please. It's quite a coincidence that this morning's spelling test is on wand warning sounds, don't you think, fairies?'

Elly and Saphie reluctantly nodded. 'Yes, Mrs Clovercloud.'

'Now hurry up and get to class,' said

their teacher, shooing them away. 'I'll be there shortly.'

Elly's heart was beating rapidly as they flew off. This must be the spelling test Saphie tried to warn her about. Elly knew she was in trouble. She couldn't remember anything about wand warning sounds. She didn't even know her wand could *make* warning sounds. This was very bad – Elly couldn't afford to fail any more tests. Out of the four tests she'd had since arriving at Mossy Blossom, she'd failed *five*. The last one had been about making rainbows and Elly had failed it so badly that Mrs Clovercloud actually failed her twice.

'I've never seen an entirely black rainbow before,' she had said, shaking her head in disbelief.

'Quick, Saphie,' Elly whispered urgently

as they slipped into their seats. 'How do I make warning sounds?'

Saphie pointed to the diamond-shaped button on the handle of her wand.

'Press this,' she said. 'Once for low-level warnings, twice for medium and lots of times for an emergency. If you hold the button down, it sends out a wand-wide distress signal. Any wands nearby will immediately make the signal, too.'

This seemed pretty straightforward. 'Thanks, Saph,' said Elly gratefully. 'I owe you.'

'There's something else, though,' said Saphie. 'You need to –'

But before she could finish, the door opened and Mrs Clovercloud appeared. 'We'll start straight away,' the teacher said briskly.

'Gabi Cruddleperry. Please demonstrate a low-level warning sound.'

Gabi stood up and pressed the purple button on the handle of her wand. A chime like a church bell rang out.

'Very good,' said Mrs Clovercloud. Gabi sat down, smiling smugly.

Primrose Petals was next. She had two very long plaits which had a habit of wriggling around like two thick snakes. If something unexpected happened, they stood straight up in the air in alarm.

Today, though, they hung sedately down her back. Primrose performed her wand sound without a hitch, as did Marabella Shimmerbliss.

'Now you, Sapphire,' said Mrs Clovercloud. 'Please demonstrate the emergency signal.'

Saphie stood up. Her warning sound was a little wobbly but Mrs Clovercloud nodded.

'Good,' she said. 'Just remember to hold the button down firmly.' Then she turned to Elly.

'Elinora,' Mrs Clovercloud said. 'Please demonstrate the wand-wide distress signal.'

Elly stood up. For once, she wasn't nervous. She'd been watching the other fairies make their signals, and it looked easy.

'The wand-wide distress signal,' she announced, and held down the blue diamond button.

Her wand made a low, rumbling sound, like distant thunder or a purring cat. Elly was puzzled. Was it supposed to sound like that? The longer Elly pressed the button, the louder and higher the noise became. Then

the wand began shaking and shuddering, like it was trying to wiggle out of Elly's hand.

Elly looked over at Saphie, who made desperate signals with her hands under the desk. Elly knew Saphie was trying to help her, but she had no idea what the hand signals meant. The noise was now like that of a giant, hungry mosquito – and a moment later, it sounded like a whole squadron of mosquitoes, because every other wand in the classroom had started making the noise, too.

'Elly,' said Mrs Clovercloud, alarmed. 'What are you doing?'

'Just what I'm meant to do,' said Elly. 'Holding down the blue diamond.'

All the students now had their hands over their ears.

'Did you install the sound crystal into the handle?' said Mrs Clovercloud.

Elly's stomach dropped. This was the first

she had heard about any sound crystal. She looked over at Saphie, who shrugged helplessly. The sound was becoming unbearable.

'Turn it off, Elly!' yelled Mrs Clovercloud.

But Elly couldn't. The blue diamond button seemed to be stuck. The wand continued shuddering until finally it jumped right out of her hand and started spinning around on the floor. A moment later, all the other wands flew from their owners' hands and joined Elly's wand on the floor.

Surely, thought Elly unhappily as the noise screamed in her ears, *it couldn't get any louder than this?*

But it did. It was as loud as an aeroplane. Then as loud as two aeroplanes. The desks started vibrating and the windows rattled.

'Do something!' cried Primrose Petals. Her

plaits were curled up very tightly around her ears, like earmuffs. 'I can't stand it!'

Elly tried desperately to jump on her wand, but it kept slipping deftly away.

Then, just when Elly thought her ears were about to peel off, there was an enormous bang followed by the sound of shattering glass. And finally, everything was quiet.

Very, very, quiet.

It stayed that way until Mrs Clovercloud's voice broke the silence.

'Elinora Knottleweed-Eversprightly!' she boomed. 'Just look what you've done!'

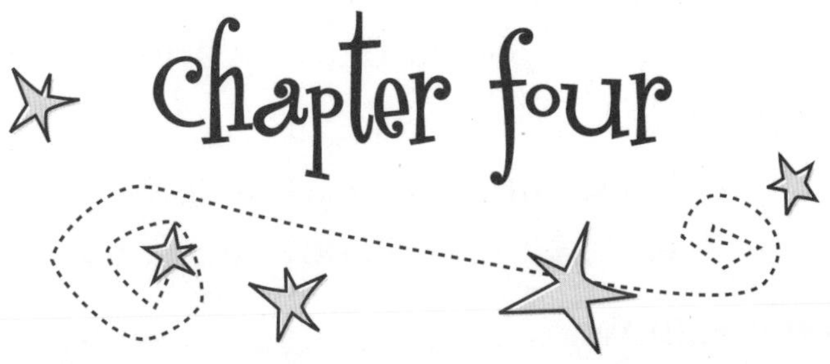

Chapter four

The classroom suddenly felt cooler and Elly soon realised why. Every window in the classroom had shattered, and a breeze was blowing through where the panes used to be. The wands lay heaped on the floor, still and silent. Primrose Petals' plaits were still curled around her ears as if they were scared the noise might come back.

Now that it was all over, some of the fairies looked like they were trying not to laugh.

But Mrs Clovercloud wasn't smiling, not even a little. Elly suspected that she'd just failed another test.

'Elly,' said Mrs Clovercloud sternly. Elly knew from Mrs Clovercloud's tone what was coming next.

'I know, I know,' she sighed, standing up. 'Go straight to the Head Fairy's office.'

Madame Silverwings' office was so familiar to Elly that the door seemed to creak in a friendly way when it opened. Madame Silverwings was seated behind a desk which hovered above the ground. When she was calm, the desk stayed close to the floor, but when she was angry the desk began rising towards the ceiling. It's bad enough being told off by someone who is looking straight at you, but it's much worse if they're yelling down at you from up high. Elly was glad to see that at the moment, the desk was quite low.

'I'm sorry to see you in here again so soon, Elly,' said Madame Silverwings as Elly sat down. 'Do you know how many times you've been sent to see me since you arrived at Mossy Blossom?'

Elly shook her head. 'A lot?' she said helpfully.

'Twenty-seven times,' stated Madame Silverwings. 'Six times for creating a disturbance in class, four of which were of an explosive nature. Nine for being late. Ten times for riding your skateboard on schoolgrounds and twice for turning a staff member purple.' Madame Silverwings looked disapproving. '*Twice*, Elly. One time might be dismissed

as an unfortunate accident, but two times is inexcusable.'

Elly thought this was unfair. After all, she hadn't *planned* to turn Miss Flufferbuff, the Synchronised Flying instructor, purple. It was her stupid wand's fault. It had puffed out a big cloud of sticky purple dust just as Miss Flufferbuff had flown by. Unfortunately, the purple dust stuck fast and poor Miss Flufferbuff had to be re-colourised.

Elly had felt very bad about it. Re-colourisation was a painful process that involved lying flat on your back in a re-colourisation chamber while thousands of tiny brushes scoured your skin. On the day Miss Flufferbuff had finished being re-colourised, Elly had waited outside with some flowers. It was just a shame that her

wand chose that moment to malfunction again, and dye Miss Flufferbuff an even deeper shade of mauve.

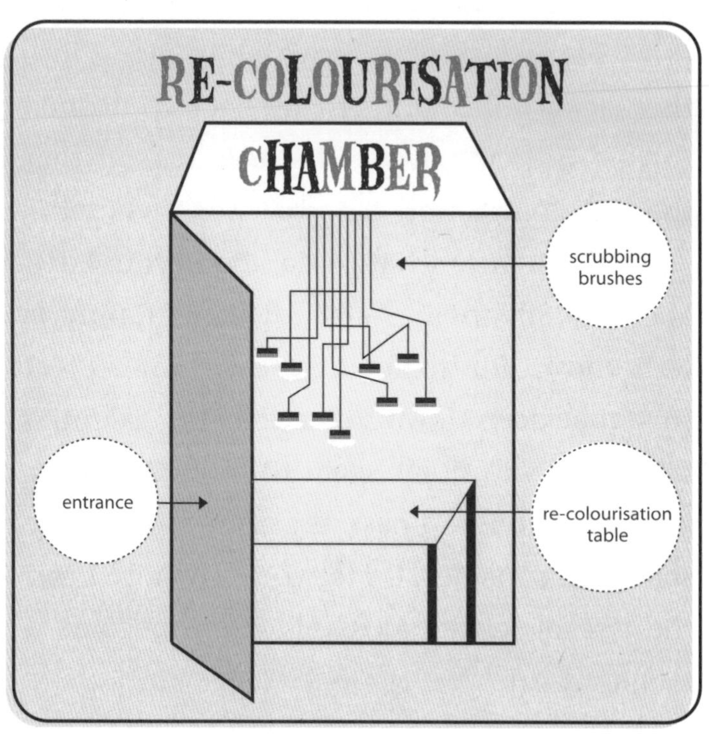

Fairies change colour very easily. Flying through a field of sunflower pollen can turn them yellow and going through a particularly dark rain cloud can turn them grey. This is useful if they wish to blend into the background, but getting back to normal can be difficult. It was for this reason that the re-colourisation chamber was invented.

'I'm not sure what to do about you, Elly,' Madame Silverwings sighed. 'Your family is well known for achieving great things. I feel sure that deep down you are a very talented fairy, but you don't seem to be taking your studies seriously. I have the reputation of the school to consider. If I let you stay here I run the risk of letting Mossy Blossom become a laughing stock.'

Madame Silverwings' desk zoomed up

close to Elly's chair, and the Head Fairy looked very intently at Elly.

'What would you do,' she asked, 'with a fairy who'd rather be a human?'

Elly didn't know what to say and so, without thinking, she blurted out the first thing that came into her head.

'I'd send her to a human school,' she said. The moment she said it she realised that this was exactly what she wanted. Elly didn't know much about human schools, but she guessed there would be no magic and no flying. That alone made them one hundred times better than fairy school.

'Oh, Elly,' said Madame Silverwings sadly. 'That's impossible. Only one or two exceptional students get sent to human schools per year. The cream of the crop.'

'Oh,' said Elly, disappointed. There was no way anyone would consider her to be the cream of the crop.

Elly started to feel a bit worried. Her mum had said that Mossy Blossom was her last chance. If she got thrown out of here, no other school would take her.

My last chance ...

The words echoed in Elly's head for a while, then made a sudden pinging sound. She'd just realised something. If no other fairy school would accept her, then surely that meant no more school! That meant sleeping in. It meant skateboarding all day. It meant no homework and no dumb school uniform. The more Elly thought about it, the more being expelled from Mossy Blossom Academy seemed like a good idea. A plan started to form in her head.

Elly put on her saddest face.

'You're right,' she sighed. 'I'm a terrible student and I probably won't get any better.'

'It sounds like you don't *want* to stay, Elly,' frowned Madame Silverwings. Her desk started to rise.

'Oh I really do,' said Elly hastily. 'I love Mossy Blossom.'

'Good,' said Madame Silverwings as the desk returned to the ground, 'because I've decided to give you a week's trial. If you make it through the next five days without making any mistakes I'll let you stay.'

'No mistakes at all?' asked Elly.

'None,' said Madame Silverwings firmly. 'If you make even *one* you'll have to leave Mossy Blossom forever.'

Elly was pleased. Her plan was working already. It would be dead easy to make a mistake in a week. After all, she made mistakes every day without even trying! Then she would be free of fairy school forever.

Madame Silverwings, of course, had no idea what Elly was plotting.

'You will have to be on your best behaviour,' she warned. 'No arriving late, no skateboarding and *definitely* no more turning teachers purple.'

Elly nodded. 'I'll be perfect,' she promised. *Perfectly terrible,* she thought silently to herself.

Chapter five

The easiest way to be expelled, Elly decided, was to ride her skateboard around. Skateboards were strictly forbidden at school and it wouldn't be long before someone caught her. But the next time she pulled her board out of her bag, all the wheels promptly fell off. Elly picked them up. They were completely worn out. This was bad news. Rainbow wheels were very expensive and very hard to come by. Her skateboard might be out of action for ages.

So that afternoon Elly had to catch the Fairy Flock home and it was terrible. Someone's wand kept jabbing into her back, and wings kept tickling her nose and making her sneeze. Elly was very relieved when she finally arrived at her stop. She quickly removed her cloud coat and tucked her wings out of view.

Elly was very happy to finally be home today. She looked around her as she walked up towards her house. *Raspberry Drive is very pretty,* she thought to herself, *but also very dull.* As far as Elly could tell, there were no other fairies living on her street.

How can you pick a fairy's house? It's easy, once you know what to look out for:

1. The garden is always green, no matter what the weather has been like.

2. All the flowers grow to exactly the same height.

3. The house often has a fancy doorknob.

4. The chimneys blow out multi-coloured smoke.

5. Fairy houses always seem to look a bit different each time you look at them, although it's hard to say why.

There were hardly any human kids living in Elly's street either, until a family moved in to the empty house next door to the Knottleweed-Eversprightlys. Elly had seen a boy in the backyard and she'd glimpsed a girl gazing out one of the windows who looked about her own age. Fairies were allowed to befriend humans so long as they never revealed their real identities. In fact, these friendships were actually encouraged, as it helped fairies discover more about humans. But there was no way Elly was going to make friends with one. She hated humans.

As far as she could see, fairies were expected to be servants to humans – granting their wishes, fixing up their dumb mistakes. What did fairies get in return? Nothing! Elly didn't see why she should be expected to help them out. Half the humans didn't even believe in fairies. The other half loved fairies way too much. Elly had heard terrible stories about fairies nearly getting squeezed to death by mobs of excited little girls. No, in Elly's opinion humans were best avoided altogether.

When Elly arrived at her own house, she felt like a snack. Quietly she tiptoed to the kitchen and peeped around the corner. The fridge was humming away quietly. It looked like a perfectly normal fridge. But it wasn't. Elly carefully put on a crash helmet. Then she took a deep breath and rushed into the room, head down. As she neared the fridge the door flung open and a large lump of mouldy, smelly cheese flew out. It splattered against her crash helmet and oozed down the sides. Elly ignored it and kept running. A moment later the fridge opened again and flung out a handful of soggy lettuce leaves. Elly tried to dodge them, but they squished across her face.

Elly sighed and peeled the leaves off. The fridge was one of her mum's latest inventions: a self-cleaning model that ejected anything past its used-by date. Elly knew that a fridge like that might be useful but why did it have to be so violent about it?

The Knottleweed-Eversprightly household was full of stuff like this, but luckily not all of it was as bad-tempered as the fridge. Elly's favourite was the bath that kept the water at the perfect temperature for as long as you were in there. It also had an inbuilt bubble-bath dispenser which offered 120 colours

of bubble bath – everything from red to purple or even gold with pink stripes. It was a singing bathtub too, with a rich, melodious voice. Sometimes Elly sang along with it, but other times she liked lying back in a lather of multi-coloured bubbles while the tub sang to her. The songs it sung depended on what mood it was in. One day it was pop songs, and the next it was country music. Elly and the bath had spent many happy hours together, and whenever she walked by it would try to convince her she needed washing.

'You are looking diiiiiiiirty,' it would warble. 'Come and take a baaaaaaaaath!'

Finally, Elly reached the fridge. She grabbed some biscuits and ran out of the kitchen as fast as she could, narrowly avoiding getting hit by a rotten tomato.

Only when she was safely out of there did she look at the biscuits. *Great*. They were her dad's healthy zucchini biscuits. Elly ate them anyway – there was no way she was dealing with that fridge again so soon.

Just as she finished, Elly's dad appeared, holding Kara with one hand and a big net with the other.

'Elly, look after Kara for me, please,' he said. 'Someone's turned all our washing into birds. I'll have to catch it all before it flies away.'

Elly looked outside. The backyard was full of birds, some of which had pegs attached to their wings. Swans, parrots and crows were perched on the line while below, a couple of seagulls that looked distinctly like Elly's underpants were squabbling over a worm.

It was obvious to Elly who'd done it.

'Bird!' exclaimed Kara, looking very pleased with herself.

Their dad handed Kara to Elly. Kara dribbled lovingly onto Elly's shoulder and a puff of smoke rose up where the drops fell. Baby-fairy dribble is very strong stuff.

'But I've got homework to do,' Elly grumbled, quickly wiping up the drool with a special reinforced hankie that she kept just for this purpose.

'Do it later,' said her dad, heading outside. 'I'm very busy.'

What else is new? thought Elly. Her parents were always busy these days. Elly could remember when they had time to take her to the park and read her stories. But that was before Kara came along, and before her mum's work became so important. Now it sometimes felt like they'd forgotten Elly even existed.

Elly put her sister down in front of her blocks, and Kara stacked them into towers. This might not sound unusual, except that Kara didn't use her hands to do it. The blocks obediently rose from the ground one by one to form the stack. When the tower got too high, it tumbled over and Kara gurgled with delight.

Elly felt a tiny stab of jealousy. *How did Kara get so good at magic without ever even going to fairy school?*

It was hard not to feel dumb around Kara. Elly's parents kept saying, 'You're just a late bloomer,' but Elly wasn't so sure. She suspected she was one of those boring plants that never flowered at all.

Elly's wand beeped. Saphie had sent her a wand-message. There was just enough power in the wand for Elly to see Saphie's face faintly in the star.

'Our homework for next week's Spelling class is learning to make a wand-trail,' Saphie reported. 'It's pretty easy. Just fill the handle with dehydrated stardust then push the purple button. A trail of stars should follow behind your wand when you wave it.' The message crackled to a finish.

Elly knew right away there was no way she'd be able to do that homework. The only thing she'd ever been able to make trail behind her wand before was a stream of toothpaste. It wasn't even a good flavour either, like Sparkle-Mint – the nice minty toothpaste that makes purple sparks burst from your mouth like fireworks as you brush. *Her* toothpaste tasted like parsley.

Of course, Elly should've been happy about all this. After all, she was trying to get expelled from Mossy Blossom, and making a parsley toothpaste trail would definitely do the trick. But watching how easily Kara did magic made Elly wish she could do it too. Was it possible that her parents were right about her being a late bloomer? Elly had some star-dust in her bag. Maybe she should just *try*

making a wand-trail.

But just as she started working, Kara got bored with her blocks and started climbing all over her big sister.

'I can't play right now,' said Elly, looking around for something to distract Kara with. Nearby was another of her mother's inventions: the Space-Case.

The Space-Case was like a flying suitcase, designed for fairies who had lots of things to carry. Air-holes in the top meant that even pets could be transported in it. The case was made from a new, top-secret material that instantly blended in with any background it flew up against, hiding the contents as well as the case itself. This was useful for avoiding human attention while flying, but it caused problems, too. Elly could never remember

where the Space-Case was, and tripped over it almost every day.

Still, it might be good for entertaining Kara – it was the perfect size for a baby to sit in. Elly looked out the window at her dad. She suspected he might not like her idea as much as she did, but luckily he was running around after a large white swan.

Elly plonked Kara inside the Space-Case. Kara gurgled delightedly.

'Fly to the other side of the room and back,' commanded Elly, and the Space-Case rose and sailed smoothly to the far wall before returning.

Kara clapped her hands. 'More!' she said.

'Fly downstairs and back,' said Elly, and the Space-Case obediently took off. Elly continued working on her wand but hadn't gotten very far when the Space-Case returned, so she sent it away to do twelve laps of the lounge room. By the next time the Space-Case returned, Elly was in a very bad mood. Her homework was not going well. Every time she tried filling the wand with stardust, it made an odd sneezing sound and all the dust blew out again.

At first the Space-Case waited patiently beside Elly, but then it started nudging her arm to get her attention. It bumped her so hard that the remaining stardust billowed into the air and floated away. Elly slammed down the wand.

'Just go AWAY!' she yelled angrily, and the Space-Case rose quickly into the air. Elly realised what she'd said.

'No! Stop! Stop!' she cried, waving her arms in the air. But it was too late. The Space-Case had already flown straight out the open window.

Elly rushed over to see where it went, imagining all kinds of terrible things. The Space-Case might fly all the way to Siberia. Or it might run out of power while over an ocean. Or it might get sucked into a black hole.

But then something much, much worse happened. Something so dreadful that Elly stared with her mouth open, unable to speak. The Space-Case sailed over the fence and straight into the open window of the new neighbours' house.

Chapter Six

Elly wasn't crazy about her sister in the way that everyone else seemed to be. She didn't go gooey over Kara's little hands and she wasn't impressed by her strange, toothless smiles. Plus, she was tired of all her hankies being full of baby-drool. Elly's life had been much better before Kara arrived.

So you might think that Elly would've been quite happy when Kara disappeared over the fence. But she wasn't. In fact, she was very upset. And it wasn't just because she knew she was going to be in big trouble when her parents found out what had happened. Something very strange had happened to Elly the moment Kara was out of sight: she started to miss her sister. Even though Kara could be annoying, she was also kind of fun. And besides, Kara was the only person Elly knew who was always happy to see her, no matter what. Elly couldn't imagine what it'd be like to come home and not hear Kara coo delightedly. So Elly didn't think twice about what to do.

Without even checking to see if the coast was clear, Elly grabbed her wand and flew over the neighbours' fence. She balanced for a moment on the ledge of the window she'd seen the Space-Case vanish into, and peered

cautiously through the curtains. She could just make out the Space-Case wedged on top of a wardrobe in the far corner of the room.

No humans seemed to be around, so Elly dropped onto the floor. She'd never been inside a human house before, although she'd seen pictures of them in her Human Studies classes. She recognised this as a bedroom, but it was very different to the fairy version. For a start, the bed was at ground level rather than hanging from the ceiling. Then when Elly sat on the chair, she was surprised that it didn't automatically adjust to her shape and height. Even more surprising was the floor rug that stayed put rather than constantly trying to sneak below her feet.

Something sparkly caught her eye. Stuck to the back of the door were hundreds of stickers of all different sizes and shapes. There were pandas and flowers, birds and rainbows. There was a row of butterflies, each slightly smaller than the one in front. Elly couldn't stop staring. She'd heard about stickers before but had never actually seen one. Everything in a fairy house is so shiny that stickers would simply refuse to stay stuck.

Just then Elly heard Kara make a sound

and she suddenly remembered why she was there. Quickly, she flew up to the Space-Case and looked inside. To her relief Kara was fast asleep and snoring. Now all she had to do was remove the case and fly back home before anyone found them here.

Elly gave the Space-Case a tug but it was wedged in tight! The tug woke Kara up, and when she saw her sister she started banging excitedly on the side of the case. The Space-Case moved a little bit. Elly bit her lip. She'd have to be careful. If the case became un-wedged when she wasn't ready, it might crash to the ground. Elly looked around for something to help with the un-wedging and felt a sharp jabbing pain in her side. Her wand.

If I was a better fairy I could use this to fix

everything, she thought, pulling the wand out of her belt. She was about to throw the wand on the ground when she had a thought. Maybe she *could* use the wand after all, but just not in the same way another fairy might use it. Carefully, she stuck the star part of the wand beneath the Space-Case and wiggled it gently, until slowly but surely the case started to come free.

It was hard work and Elly's arm soon began aching. Inside the case Kara giggled and smiled as if this was all part of a game. With a loud creak, the Space-Case finally came loose. It teetered for a moment on the edge of the wardrobe, then it slipped through Elly's hands and hurtled towards the floor.

'Fly to the bed!' she shouted in her most

commanding voice. Her heart was pounding. The Space-Case screeched to a halt only centimetres from the ground, then much to Elly's relief started to rise again. Moments later it came to rest gently on the bed. Elly flew down beside it and unclipped the top. Out popped Kara.

'I'm *sooo* glad to see you!' said Elly, lifting her out and hugging her.

'Thanks!' said a voice. Elly looked at Kara in surprise. When did she learn to speak? Then the voice added, 'I'm happy to see you, too ... except I don't know who you are.'

Elly spun around. Standing in the doorway was the human girl she'd glimpsed through the window the other day. Her arms were crossed and she had closed the door behind her. Elly gulped.

This is going to be very tricky to explain, she thought.

Chapter Seven

There is a chapter in the Fairy Code about what to do if a human catches you in their house. This is what it says:

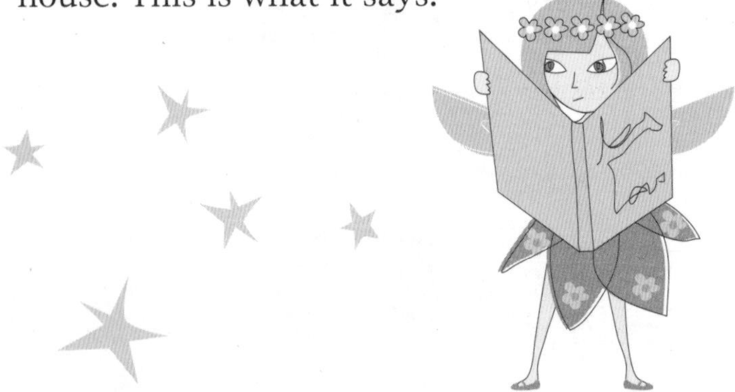

1. DON'T GET CAUGHT!

This is such an important rule that it takes up an entire page all of its own.

On the next page it goes on to say:

2.
Never enter human houses unless you are there on official fairy business.
3.
Never perform magic for your human neighbours.
4.
Never **EVER** let a human see your wings.

These rules are so important that they appear everywhere in fairy schools. They are written on all the blackboards and they are printed on every school bag. Fairies are made to recite them every morning at assembly. Even Elly knew them off by heart. So when she saw the human girl standing in the doorway she was horrified to realise that she'd already managed to break most of the rules.

Elly's mind started ticking over the various ways she could deal with this situation. The first thing she thought of was grabbing Kara and flying out the window, and pretending none of this actually happened. But there were some problems with this plan. The human girl would probably watch where Elly went and then she'd tell everyone she lived next to a fairy. Elly's next idea was to make up a lie about what she was doing in her neighbours' house. But what lie could she possibly concoct that explained her wings, her sister's wings and the Space-Case? Elly would need a week to think of a way to explain all that.

So this left Elly with only one option: tell the truth.

She didn't really like this option, especially as she vaguely remembered hearing that once you reveal your true identity to a human you had to be their servant forever. But Elly had run out of ideas. Maybe not all humans knew about the 'servant forever' bit.

Elly looked at the girl and smiled nervously. 'I guess you want me to tell you what I'm doing here,' she said.

The girl didn't smile back. 'That would be nice,' she replied.

Elly took a deep breath. The quicker she got this over with the better.

'I'm a fairy,' she said, in a rush. Then she waited for the girl to start squealing and jumping around with excitement. But the girl stayed exactly where she was. Elly was puzzled. Perhaps she hadn't heard her.

'I'm a fairy,' repeated Elly loudly, waving her wand in the air, 'and my sister here is a fairy too. She accidentally flew over here in a suitcase and I flew in after her.' Elly looked at the girl. Surely she'd heard that.

The girl looked at her thoughtfully.

'Are you going to fly back through my window when you leave?' she said eventually.

'Probably,' said Elly cautiously. It seemed

like a weird question. Maybe the girl was waiting for all of her little human friends to come over so they could squeeze her to death together.

The girl went over to the window and opened it as wide as she could. Then she faced Elly. ‘OK then,’ she said, pointing at the window. ‘Let’s see you do it.’

Elly couldn’t believe it. She had been warned over and over that if a human caught you they’d never stop pestering you for wishes. But it seemed like this girl just wanted Elly to leave. It just didn’t make sense.

Then something dawned on Elly. ‘You don’t believe I’m a fairy, do you?’ she said to the girl.

The girl shrugged. ‘I’ll believe you when you fly out the window.’

Fine, thought Elly. *If that's what I have to do.*

She stood on the edge of the bed and leapt into the air, arms outstretched. *This should set things straight pretty quickly.* Elly rose up into the air …

… and promptly fell to the floor. Elly remembered the zucchini biscuits she'd eaten. If you fly too soon after eating, you sometimes get a cramp.

The human girl was grinning.

'Don't laugh,' said Elly crossly. 'I really can fly.'

'*Sure* you can,' said the girl. 'And I bet your little sister can too.'

'Of course she can't,' said Elly haughtily. 'She's way too young. But I can, usually. I've just got a cramp.'

'Look,' said the human girl, 'I've got stuff to do. I'm really not interested in playing your dumb little make-believe game. There are plenty of other girls around here who love fairies. Go and pester them instead.'

Elly had heard about humans like this, of course, but she never imagined she'd actually meet one.

'It's not just that you don't believe I'm a fairy, is it?' Elly said. 'You don't believe in fairies at *all*, do you?'

'No,' said the human girl. 'I don't.'

So Elly decided to play a trick on this irritating human. She clutched her heart dramatically and fell to the ground.

'Don't you know what happens when a human child says she doesn't believe in fairies?' she moaned faintly, closing her eyes. 'One of us disappears, instantly.'

Then she waited for the girl to come rushing over. But nothing happened. Eventually, Elly opened one eye. The girl was sitting at her desk, reading a book.

Elly gave up. Quite clearly this girl was completely heartless. Elly may as well pack up and head home. But just then she heard a funny sound, which was closely followed by a bad smell. At first Elly just assumed that both the noise and smell were coming from Kara, but when she turned around she saw that something much more serious was happening. Blue sparks were shooting out of the Space-Case, closely followed by puffs of evil-smelling smoke. Something was horribly wrong.

Elly stared in horror. She knew how proud her mum was of the Space-Case. How would she react when she found out that Elly had broken it? Elly realised that tears were rolling down her cheeks. There was probably some Fairy Code rule about not getting upset in front of a human, but right now Elly didn't care. She let the tears roll.

'Hey,' said the girl awkwardly. 'Don't cry. It's OK.'

Elly shook her head. 'You don't understand. I've broken my mum's invention. I'm in so much trouble.'

The girl came and sat beside Elly. 'Don't worry.' Her voice was much friendlier now. 'I might not like fairies but I'll tell you what I do like: machines. I bet I can fix this contraption for you.'

Elly stopped crying and looked at the girl. She really wanted to believe her. But it was hard to imagine that this skinny little kid with pigtails and freckles would be able to fix something as complicated as the Space-Case. On the other hand, she didn't seem like the average sort of girl that Elly had learnt about in Human Studies. Perhaps she should just trust her.

'What's your name?' asked Elly.

'Jess,' replied the girl. 'Jess Chester.' Then she smiled. It was a good sort of smile.

The sort that used her eyes as well as her mouth. It made you want to smile right back, which Elly did.

'Well, Jess Chester,' Elly said, 'it's lucky for me that you don't believe in fairies, because I'll owe you about a billion wishes if you fix this thing.'

chapter eight

Jess rummaged through a desk drawer and produced a set of tools that looked like they'd been made especially for her. They were just the right size to fit in her hand and had bright, jewel-coloured handles. The tools made Jess look less like a kid and more like a mechanic. But even so, Elly wasn't holding out much hope that Jess would actually fix the Space-Case.

The case was still on the bed, sparking

and vibrating. It made low, groaning sounds, like someone with a terrible toothache. Elly stood as far away from it as possible, holding Kara tightly to her chest, but Jess confidently flipped the case over and undid a little panel on the base. A cloud of stinky, yellow smoke puffed out. Jess waved it away and shone a torch inside while Elly watched anxiously. If Jess couldn't fix the Space-Case, what was she going to do?

Jess started poking around inside the Space-Case with a finger. At first she looked puzzled, and then the puzzlement turned rapidly to astonishment. She turned and stared at Elly.

'What? WHAT?' said Elly frantically. *There must be something terribly wrong!*

'You really *are* a fairy,' whispered Jess.

Elly rolled her eyes. 'That's what I've been trying to tell you!' she said. 'Why do you suddenly believe me now?'

Jess pointed to the Space-Case. 'This engine. I've never seen anything like it before,' she said, her voice full of awe. 'I mean, it's not just new technology, it's un-*dreamt*-of technology. It's like it was made by ... well, by magic.'

Elly didn't like the sound of this. 'Does that mean you can't fix it?' she asked anxiously.

'Oh, I can fix it,' said Jess confidently. 'It's just got water in it.' She tipped it upside down and a clear, sparkly liquid came dribbling out onto the floor. Elly recognised it at once. Baby-fairy drool.

Jess adjusted a couple of things. then put the cover back on the Space-Case. The sparking and the smoking had stopped, but Elly was still not convinced it would actually work.

Jess smiled at her. 'Go on,' she said. 'Test it out. I'm dying to see what it does.'

Elly took a deep breath. 'Fly around the room,' she commanded.

The Space-Case rose from the bed and began to fly around. It was hard to tell who was more astonished – Jess or Elly.

'Now loop-the-loop,' said Elly, and the

case obediently did three perfect loops. 'You fixed it!' she cried, jumping up and down on the bed.

'Wow,' said Jess, impressed. 'That's a pretty cool suitcase.'

'Is there anything I can do for you in return?' Elly asked. She was suddenly a bit nervous. If Jess knew anything about fairies, this would be when she brought up the thing about being a human's servant forever.

But Jess just laughed. 'Don't worry,' she said. 'It was fun. Got anything else that needs fixing?'

Elly's wand chose that moment to start spluttering and coughing.

'What about that thing? It sounds sick,' said Jess, pointing at the wand.

Elly looked at the wand, too. She

wasn't sure if she wanted it fixed. Having a broken wand would help her get expelled from Mossy Blossom. The wand coughed again and began shivering. Then before Elly could stop her, Jess had it in her hand.

'The poor thing,' she said sympathetically. 'It's not very well.'

Elly rolled her eyes. 'It's just pretending to get your attention,' she said.

But Jess opened up the wand's handle and began examining its insides. The wand whimpered and Elly started feeling guilty. Maybe it wasn't pretending after all.

'Is it OK?' she said, peering over Jess's shoulder.

Jess frowned. 'It's weird. The central supporting strut looks like it's been eaten

away by some kind of acid. It's about to snap in two!'

Elly looked at Kara. She was fairly sure she knew what had caused the problem. She reached out for the wand.

'Thanks,' she said. 'I'll take it to a wand-mechanic.'

But Jess had a determined gleam in her eye. 'Hang on – I think I can fix it,' she said, scrabbling around in a drawer. She pulled out a blue pen and a couple of rubber bands.

'It'll probably be a quick fix,' she added. 'But better than nothing.'

'Really, don't bother,' said Elly, but she could see that there was no point trying to stop Jess.

She removed the damaged strut, which instantly snapped in two. Then she wiggled the pen into place. A few moments later she handed the wand back to Elly. Her eyes were bright.

'I'm *really* not sure about this,' Jess said, 'but let's see if it works.'

Elly pressed the purple button, held the wand up in the air and waited.

And waited.

The longer she waited, the more relieved she felt. Jess hadn't managed to fix the wand after all.

'What's supposed to happen?' asked Jess, looking around.

'It's supposed to make a trail of stars when I wave it,' said Elly, trying not to look too happy that it hadn't worked.

'But you haven't waved it yet, have you?' Jess pointed out. 'You're holding it still.'

'Oh yeah,' said Elly, feeling silly. It was embarrassing when a human knew more about wands than a fairy did. Elly swished

the wand through the air and as she did, a trail of silver stars blossomed out behind, hanging in the air for a moment before dissolving into even smaller bursts of stars.

Elly had thought she didn't want the wand to work. She'd decided that having a faulty wand would be the easiest way to get thrown out of Mossy Blossom. But she couldn't help being very excited when she saw the wand-trail streaming out behind her wand. It was the first time one of her spells had actually worked properly. It felt good. Really good.

'You're the best!' she said, and hugged Jess. 'I knew you could fix it.'

'Let go, you're strangling me!' said Jess, but she looked pleased. 'I'm glad it's working, but don't forget, it might not be for long. You should get it repaired properly.'

There was another whimpering noise and both girls stared at the wand. Was there something else the matter with it? Then Elly realised it wasn't the wand, it was Kara. She looked hungry and tired. Elly knew she'd better get her home soon – before her dad got worried. She scooped Kara up and turned to Jess.

'If there's ever anything you want to wish for, just ask me,' Elly said. It was a big promise to make, but she really meant it.

Jess smiled. 'Thanks,' she said, 'but from what I can see, the human way of solving problems is much more reliable than the fairy way.'

Chapter nine

That night Elly started worrying about what she'd said to Jess. She was pretty sure that the Fairy Code would strongly disapprove of promising humans any wish they wanted. Humans had a bad habit of saying things like, 'I wish you would grant all my wishes, forever.'

At first Elly comforted herself by thinking, *How much could a small human girl like Jess possibly wish for, anyway?* But it didn't take

THINGS FAIRIES KNOW ABOUT HUMANS

(that humans don't know about themselves)

1\. Humans are terrible at making wishes. They always try to wish for too much and end up worse off than they were before.

2\. Humans could understand most animal languages if they listened properly.

3\. One in every thousand humans can actually fly but have never tried. (Unfortunately these humans tend to be the ones who are scared of heights.)

her long to realise that the answer might be A LOT.

She might wish for a golden palace or a magic carpet. She might wish for something small, but complicated and fiddly, like a talking goldfish. But the biggest problem was that whatever the wish – big or small – Elly wouldn't know how to grant it. And besides, unlicensed fairies weren't even allowed to grant wishes.

There was something else that was troubling Elly. Trying to be the worst student at Mossy Blossom Academy was going to be much harder now that Jess had fixed her wand. Elly might actually have to work at making a mistake.

Elly's big chance to mess up came during the Synchronised Flying class the next day.

Elly was terrible at Synchronised Flying and ever since being dyed purple, Miss Flufferbuff, the instructor, had watched Elly very warily. Elly had trouble remembering what all the different moves were and she always ended up crashing into someone. More than once during a complicated flying routine, her wings had become tangled with another fairy's and most of the class had ended up in a tangled mess on the ground.

But all that seemed to have changed, and that day Elly didn't crash into anyone.

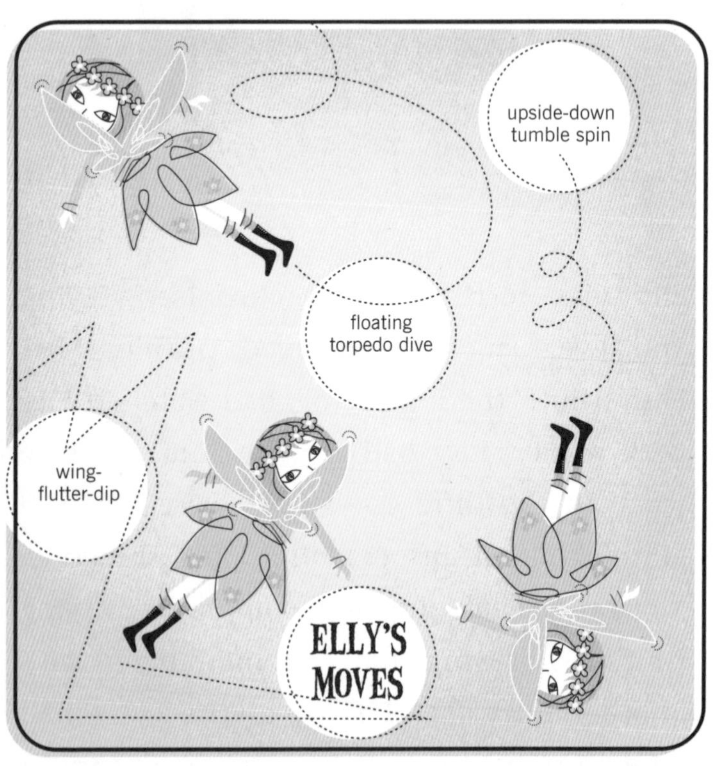

She did the wing-flutter-dip perfectly. She performed two upside-down tumble spins without feeling dizzy. And Miss Flufferbuff even praised her floating torpedo dive, saying it was one of the best she'd seen in ages.

'I don't understand,' Elly whispered to Saphie. 'I can't seem to make a mistake.'

Saphie couldn't help laughing.

'You were bad at being good,' she said, 'but now you're bad at being bad!'

At the end of the class, Miss Flufferbuff flew over and put a (still slightly purple) hand on Elly's shoulder.

'Madame Silverwings told me you were on trial this week, Elly,' she said, smiling. 'I can see you're making a big effort to improve.'

There was nothing Elly could do but smile back weakly and nod.

After school Elly changed into her jeans and tucked her wings below her favourite stripy T-shirt. She looked like an ordinary human kid.

Then she climbed over the fence and walked up to Jess's window. She could see Jess inside, sitting at her desk and frowning. Elly knocked on the window and Jess helped her in.

'What's wrong?' asked Elly.

Jess didn't look happy at all. 'I've got a project due,' she said gloomily. 'My teacher has given me until 5.30 today to finish it.'

Elly nodded sympathetically. She knew all about not getting work done in time. 'Have you got much more to do?' she asked.

Jess sighed despairingly. 'I haven't even *started*! And Mr Crankle said it's got to be really outstanding or he won't accept it at all.'

Elly already knew how smart Jess was. 'I bet you could easily do something really excellent,' she said.

But Jess shook her head. 'I'm not so sure,' she said. 'The project is about volcanoes and all the books at school are out. Plus, our computer is broken so I can't even use the internet.' She slumped in her chair. 'I'm going to fail for sure.'

Elly didn't know what the internet was, but she knew the feeling Jess was describing all too well. It was funny, though. When she found herself in the situation Jess was now in, Elly never knew how to fix it. But right now, she knew exactly what Jess should do.

'Why don't you actually *make* a volcano?' she suggested. 'You won't need books for that. And your teacher wanted something that stood out, didn't he?'

Jess was doubtful. 'He said *outstanding*, not something that stood out. Anyway, I don't know how to make a volcano. Unless you could make one with magic?' she added, looking hopefully at Elly.

'Probably not a good idea,' said Elly quickly. 'Like you said yesterday – the human way seems more reliable than the fairy way when it comes to problem-solving.' Elly had done a spelling test on turning mountains into molehills once. It hadn't gone well. She had accidentally turned a molehill into a mountain, complete with enormous, angry moles. She didn't want anything to do with magic mountains for some time.

'I guess you're right,' said Jess sadly.

Elly could see that Jess was about to give up. 'There must be some stuff lying around that we could use,' she urged.

Jess didn't look very sure at all but she started thinking. 'Well,' she said after a minute, 'there's some chicken wire in the shed which we could use as a frame.'

Elly nodded encouragingly, and Jess thought a bit more. 'We could cover the frame in clay. My mum does pottery so there's heaps in the shed.' Jess started looking excited.

'Hey!' she said. 'I could make a little gizmo so it looked like the volcano was erupting! But it'd need lava – something red and sticky.' Jess jumped up. 'Let's check the fridge.'

Elly was impressed by how bravely Jess walked through the kitchen and over to the fridge. Elly followed a few steps behind, waiting for the fridge to start firing food at them and wishing she'd brought her crash-helmet. But the fridge door remained closed, and even when Jess opened it up the contents of the Chester's fridge stayed put.

'Doesn't your fridge self-clean?' Elly asked.

Jess laughed. 'I wish. We have to clean it ourselves,' she said.

'You're so lucky,' sighed Elly.

Nothing in the fridge was quite right for lava. The raspberry jam was too thick and the tomato sauce smelled funny. There was some strawberry topping that might've been perfect, but there was only a small amount of it left.

Then Elly had a brainwave.

'Start building the frame,' she said, climbing out the window. 'I'll be back in a minute with some perfect lava.'

Back in her own house, she went straight to the bathroom. The bath was in an opera mood.

'Come to take a baaaaaath?' it trilled hopefully.

'Not right now,' said Elly apologetically, filling up a container with red bubble bath from the dispenser.

'What are you doing with thaaaaaaaat?' carolled the bath.

'I'm turning it into lava,' explained Elly.

'Sounds verrrrrrrry messy!' sang the bath excitedly.

'I'll take a bath if I get so much as a speck on me,' promised Elly.

Jess had already made the frame by the time Elly returned, so together they started covering it with clay. Elly had never used clay before. She loved how squishy it was and before long there was almost as much clay on Elly as there was on the volcano. *At least the bath will be happy to see me*, she thought.

She soon got even messier. She painted

the volcano green while Jess made a motor for the lava using the red bubble bath, rubber bands and some cogs. When Jess had finished, she put her contraption inside the volcano.

'Here goes!' said Jess.

The volcano gurgled and grumbled and all of a sudden the bubble bath came spilling over the top.

'It's good ...' said Elly slowly.

'But it's not quite right, is it?' agreed Jess. 'It needs smoke. What can we add that will do that?'

For a moment Elly was stumped. What could they possibly use that wouldn't involve setting the volcano on fire?

Then she had an idea. She felt around in her pocket and sure enough, her hankie was in there, still sodden from mopping up Kara's drool. Elly squeezed the hankie over the top of the volcano and a single, glistening drop of baby drool dropped into it. Instantly a big puff of smoke billowed up.

Jess hugged her excitedly. 'You are a genius!' she said.

Elly went bright red. She'd never been called a genius before.

And then she noticed the time. 5.15.

'Jess, how far away is your school?' she asked urgently.

'Twenty minutes on my bike,' replied Jess. 'Why?'

Elly pointed at the clock.

'Oh no!' wailed Jess in dismay. 'We'll never make it. All that hard work for nothing.'

But Elly wasn't ready to give up just yet, not when they'd come so close. She thought quickly about their options. They could catch the bus, but who knew when that might arrive? They could ask Jess's mum for a ride, but even by car they probably wouldn't make it. No, there was only one sure-fire way to make it to Jess's school by the 5.30 deadline, and it was pretty risky. If Elly got caught, she'd be in as much trouble as it was possible for a fairy to be in. Was it worth the risk?

Elly looked at Jess and then back at the volcano. It only took her a moment to decide.

'Wait here,' she said to Jess, scrambling out the window again. 'And don't worry. It's going to be OK.'

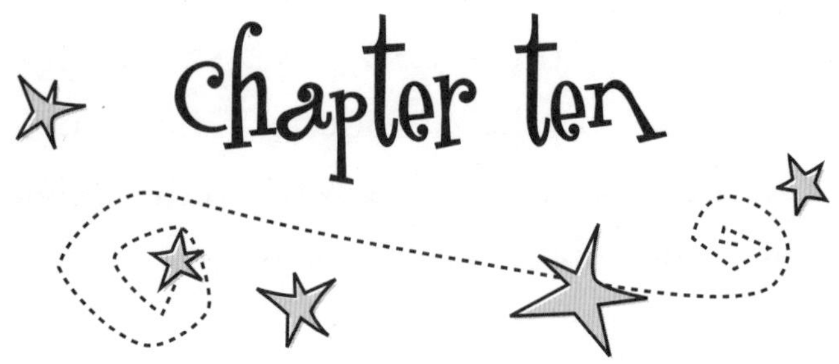

chapter ten

As she hurried along, Elly found herself thinking some very strange thoughts. She had often heard other fairies talking about the feeling that comes with granting a human wish. 'It makes you glad to be a fairy,' they'd said.

Elly always wrinkled her nose when she heard that. How could being a servant make you feel good? Yet here she was, rushing around crazily and possibly getting herself

into all kinds of trouble just for some human who she hardly knew.

But, she reminded herself, *I haven't even used any magic to help Jess. So I'm not really being a fairy.* Then a really weird thought popped into her head. *Maybe it feels good helping Jess just because she's my friend?* Elly almost laughed when she thought that. She'd never dreamt that one day she might have a *human* for a friend.

Jess was waiting anxiously when Elly returned with the Space-Case. Jess guessed straight away what she was planning. 'Are we going to ride to school on that?' she asked.

'*You're* going to ride on it,' said Elly. 'We'll put the volcano inside it and I'll fly in front.'

Jess hesitated. 'But you can't *really* fly,

can you?' she said. 'I mean, I believe you're a fairy, I just wasn't sure about the flying bit.'

Elly gave her wings a bit of a twitch. They felt fine today – no sign of a cramp. Without saying a word she rose up into the air, flew around the room and landed back in front of Jess.

'Cool!' laughed Jess, and gave one of Elly's wings a sharp tug.

'OW!' said Elly. 'What did you do that for?'

'I wanted to see if they were real,' grinned Jess, 'or just some other weird gadget of yours.'

The next task was to pack the volcano carefully inside the Space-Case. Then they carried it out to the backyard, ready for flight.

Jess was excited. 'I hope someone from

school sees me flying!' she said.

Elly shook her head. 'No-one's allowed to see us. You're not supposed to even know I'm a fairy.' Elly put on her cloud coat. 'This will disguise me and the Space-Case will hide the volcano. But I don't have anything to cover you. We'll have to just hope no-one looks up.'

'Don't worry,' said Jess, climbing onto the Space-Case. 'Everyone will be hurrying home from work. I bet they don't notice anything.'

'I hope so,' said Elly. 'I really do.'

Flying is one of those things that sounds much easier than it really is. Most humans at some stage or another think they can do it. Generally they are wrong. It's just as well, too, because most of them would hate it. Flying is very tiring, particularly when it's windy. Ever wondered why birds go to bed so early? It's because they're exhausted from flying around all day.

But Jess was excited anyway. Besides, flying wouldn't be tiring for her because all she had to do was hold on tight to the Space-Case. Or at least that was what she thought. She didn't realise how slippery the Space-Case was. Taking off was particularly tricky and Jess almost slid right off the back as they launched into the air. Luckily, she managed to grab onto one of the handles at the last minute and scramble back on.

'See if you can keep up!' called Elly, zooming on ahead.

After a couple of minutes Jess looked like she had started to get the hang of flying. She had flown in a plane before, but this was

much more fun. The Space-Case zipped along, dodging trees and powerlines and catching gusts of wind that pushed it along even more quickly. It swooped down to where a cat was snoozing on a roof, whooshing by so fast that the cat's fur parted down its back.

'Hi, cat!' called Jess. The cat watched them zoom off with a very astonished expression.

Way down below, they could see people

scurrying around. As Jess had predicted, everyone was too busy going home to pay any attention to what was going on above.

'Fly closer to the street,' she whispered to the Space-Case, and the case promptly descended until Jess was almost close enough to tap people on their heads with her toes. She grinned cheekily.

The Space-Case seemed to be enjoying itself too, getting dangerously close to someone's head then dashing around a corner if they started turning around. Jess was enjoying herself so much that she almost didn't notice that they were heading straight for a small boy holding a big red balloon.

'Careful!' called Jess in alarm, and the Space-Case tried to dodge but it was too late.

Jess's foot snagged on the string and as they darted away, she tugged the balloon right out of the boy's hand.

'Hey!' he said indignantly. 'That girl stole my balloon.'

His mother looked around. 'What girl?' she said.

'That girl in the sky,' said the boy, pointing.

But of course by then Jess and the Space-Case were out of sight. Jess managed to hurriedly untangle the balloon, and then she and the Space-Case dashed off to catch up with Elly.

At 5.25, Elly and Jess landed in the playground of South Street School. They quickly unpacked the volcano, and the Space-Case rapidly blended into a nearby bush. Then Jess led the way to her classroom.

Through the window they saw Jess's teacher, Mr Crankle. They had arrived just in time – he was packing up.

Jess picked up the volcano. 'Wait here,' she whispered, hurrying in, 'and wish me luck!'

Elly decided to explore Jess's school. She remembered telling Madame Silverwings that she would like to go to a human school. Did she really mean it? What would it be like? It certainly looked very different to a fairy school. Lining the walls were lots of kids' paintings – pictures of their pets, their families and their holidays. Elly thought they were beautiful. Fairy school kids are hardly ever allowed to paint because it's so messy. There are fairy smocks, of course, to protect their clothes, but fairies aren't supposed to get their smocks dirty either. Elly peered through a door marked 'Gym' and saw a room full of colourful mats and sports equipment. Elly sighed. The only gyms that you found at a fairy school were wing-gyms, which were filled with boring machines to help you strengthen your wings for flying.

Back in the corridor, Elly saw something that made her gasp. It was a sign, and on it was written:

No flying down the corridor!
Walk slowly.

Elly wished there were signs like this in her school. *Jess is so lucky to go to a school like this,* she thought enviously.

A few moments later, Jess came bursting out of the classroom. She was very red in the face.

'What's wrong?' asked Elly, worried. 'Didn't Mr Crankle like it?'

Jess shook her head. 'He didn't just *like* it. He *loved* it! He said it was the most original thing he'd seen all day. He wants to enter it in the science fair.'

'So why do you look like you're about to cry?' said Elly, puzzled.

'Because I'm excited. And happy,' Jess said, laughing. 'And it's all because you granted my wish.'

Elly looked at her in surprise. 'I didn't grant your wish,' she said.

'Yes, you did,' Jess insisted. 'Before you came over I was wishing that something

would happen so my assignment would be finished,' she said. 'And now it is. You're an excellent fairy.'

Elly didn't know what to say. Had she actually managed to grant someone's wish? And if so, how come it felt so much better than she'd ever imagined it would?

Chapter eleven

Elly woke up the next morning right in the middle of a dilemma. Elly had always thought that a dilemma sounded like a rather nice, snuggly thing to be in – a bit like a warm bed on a cold night. But now that she was actually in one, she realised it wasn't quite so nice after all.

Only a couple of days ago, everything had been so clear. She wanted to leave Mossy Blossom Academy, and stop being a fairy forever. But helping Jess yesterday had made her feel differently about everything. Elly had granted her first ever wish and been told that she was an excellent fairy. It was very weird to have someone say that to her. Elly was much more used to being told exactly the opposite.

And it had made her think.

First she thought: *Perhaps helping humans wouldn't be so bad, if they were like Jess?*

And then she thought: *Maybe granting wishes would be fun if I could grant them in my own way?*

But although these were good thoughts, Elly knew it wasn't as simple as that. If she wanted to become a fairy, she had to graduate from a fairy school and get her Fairy Licence. But right now she wasn't sure she could last another day at fairy school, let alone three more years.

Elly was in the dilemma all through breakfast, and she was still in it when she joined the Fairy Flock. She was so deep in her dilemma that it took her a moment to notice she was flying next to Gabi Cruddleperry.

'Ready for the test today?' smirked Gabi. 'I can't wait to see what your dumb old wand will do this time.'

Elly looked down at her wand, which was making a happy, purring sound. Jess had made her feel guilty for not treating it very well so Elly had given it a thorough clean and had straightened out some of its kinks. It was even fully charged for once.

'My wand is exactly the same as yours, Gabi,' Elly said crossly. First year students

had to use a standard, school-issued wand. It came with none of the fancy attachments that newer, more expensive wands did but it was considered important to learn magic on simple wands first.

But Gabi shook her head. 'You're wrong, Elly,' she said, pulling out a brand new wand. 'They're totally different.'

Elly gasped. The Twinkle-izer 480! This was such a famous brand that even she recognised it. Only licensed fairies were supposed to use them. Elly could guess how Gabi got hers. Her parents owned Wand World – the biggest wand shop in Fairydom – and Gabi was very spoilt.

It was an impressive-looking wand with a slick, silver handle and a star that flashed different colours as it moved. Instead of

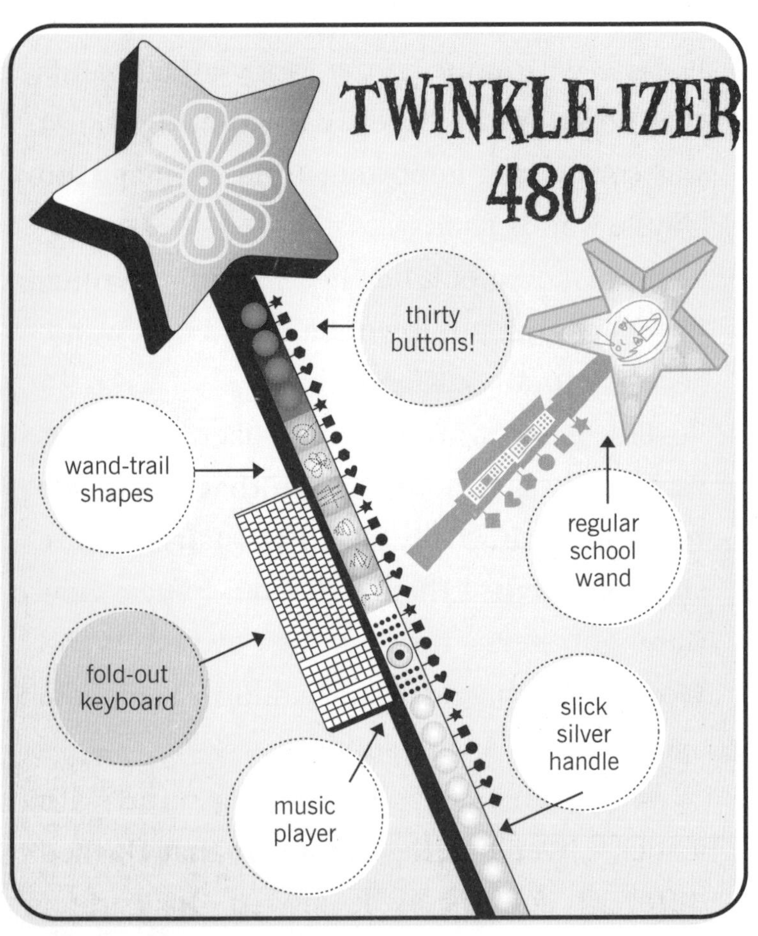
TWINKLE-IZER 480
thirty buttons!
wand-trail shapes
regular school wand
fold-out keyboard
slick silver handle
music player

the school wand's seven basic buttons the Twinkle-izer 480 had thirty. There was a small keyboard that folded out so you could type in more complicated instructions. It even played music.

'Do you know how to use it?' Elly asked. The only downside of the Twinkle-izer 480 was that it was very complicated.

'Of course!' bragged Gabi. 'It's not that hard if you're an experienced fairy. Wait till you see the wand-trails it makes.' She showed Elly a display window on the handle with lots of different wand-trail shapes pre-programmed into it.

'I just click the shape I want and the wand makes a trail,' explained Gabi, scrolling through hundreds of tiny pictures. Some of the shapes seemed very strange to Elly,

like footballs and bananas. Who would want lots of tiny bananas trailing along behind their wand?

Elly tightened her grip on her own wand. She hadn't practised making trails since Jess had done the repairs. Would it still be working when it was time for Mrs Clovercloud's class? If it wasn't, she would probably be thrown out of school. But was this a good thing or a bad thing? Elly realised she was right back in

the middle of her dilemma again.

Saphie was already in class when Elly arrived at Mossy Blossom. 'Are you ready for the test?' she whispered. 'This wand-trail thing is much more difficult than I thought.'

But Elly didn't get a chance to answer, because just then Mrs Clovercloud flew in.

'We'll start the test immediately,' she said briskly. 'Primrose Petals, you're first.'

Primrose stood up, looking nervous. Her plaits twitched slightly as she swished her wand through the air. A trail of stars appeared in its wake, but they weren't silver. They were green. And instead of fading away gently they made a loud popping sound and smelled strongly of soap.

Mrs Clovercloud sighed.

'Primrose, I think you may have put dish-

washing liquid in your wand by mistake. You'll need to work on that for next week.'

Primrose sat down, her plaits hanging dejectedly. 'Yes, Mrs Clovercloud.'

Gabi was next. Elly nudged Saphie. 'Check out her wand,' she whispered, and Saphie's eyes widened when she saw it. Elly leant forward. She was curious to see how well the new wand performed.

Gabi held the wand up high so that everyone could see that it was a Twinkle-izer 480. Then she swished it with a flourish.

Everyone waited for stars to appear. But they didn't. Instead, a herd of tiny piglets emerged, running around in circles above Gabi's head, oinking madly. The pigs didn't fade away, either. If anything, they grew bigger and brighter.

'Gabi,' said Mrs Clovercloud, 'What *are* you doing?'

Gabi started swishing the pigs away from her face, looking puzzled and annoyed. 'I'm sorry, Mrs Clovercloud,' she said, flustered. 'I must've pressed the wrong button. Let me try again.' She pressed another button and a trail of tiny puppies tumbled into the air, yapping and waggling their tails. When the piglets saw the puppies they started squealing in fright.

'Those wands are banned at school, Gabi,' said Mrs Clovercloud disapprovingly. 'Where is your school-issued one?'

'Just give me one more chance,' begged Gabi, pressing again. The next trail was made of tiny scissors that quickly joined the chase, snapping open and shut like they were trying to cut the tails off the piglets and the puppies. The classroom had become very noisy. Elly and Saphie looked at each other and tried not to laugh.

But Mrs Clovercloud had had enough. 'Take all these trails outside immediately,' she said crossly.

'Yes, Mrs Clovercloud,' said Gabi meekly. She fled from the room with the piglets, puppies and scissors trailing along behind her.

Mrs Clovercloud looked around fiercely. 'Is there *anyone* here who can do this spell correctly?' she said.

There was a silence. No-one wanted to volunteer. Then a whisper went around the room. Someone must have put up their hand. Elly looked around to see who it was and realised it was her. 'I think I know, Mrs Clovercloud,' Elly found herself saying.

'Really? *You*?' asked Mrs Clovercloud dubiously. 'I'm tired of having my time wasted.'

Elly nodded. 'Yes, Mrs Clovercloud. I'm pretty sure,' she said, although inside she wasn't sure at all. She stood up. Everyone was watching and Elly knew they were waiting for something to go wrong.

'I can't watch!' moaned Primrose, her plaits covering her eyes.

Elly took a deep breath and swished the wand through the air. A trail of perfect, silvery stars followed behind. They lingered for a moment, shimmering and twinkling, until they gently faded away.

'Ooooh!' said the class in unison.

Elly pressed the button again, this time twirling the wand in a loop so that the stars curled out and floated in a spiral towards the roof.

'Aaaah!' said the class.

Even Mrs Clovercloud seemed impressed. 'Elly,' she said, 'these are wonderful wand-trails. Show us again so that everyone else can learn.'

But the moment Elly waved her wand again she knew something was wrong. There was a twanging sound closely followed by a splintering sound. Suddenly the air was full of a weird blue mist, and all around her, fairies were shrieking and ducking under their tables.

Elly looked around in confusion. It was raining inside, and the rain was blue. And sticky. She looked at her hands and was shocked to see that they were totally blue. Her wand was blue too, and as Elly stared she realised that blue stuff was oozing out of a big crack in the handle. Finally it dawned on her what had happened. The pen Jess had put inside her wand must have broken.

The blue rain was actually ink. Elly didn't have a good feeling about this.

Slowly, she turned to look at Mrs Clovercloud. She had learnt something about her teacher very early on. When she was cross her cheeks went bright pink. When she was furious, they went scarlet. Right now, though, it was hard to tell if Mrs Clovercloud was cross or furious because her cheeks were blue. Her nose was blue too. And her ears? All blue. In fact, Mrs Clovercloud was blue from head to toe. But even without being able to see the real colour of her cheeks, Elly had the feeling that she knew exactly what sort of a mood Mrs Clovercloud was in.

And it wasn't a good one.

Chapter Twelve

If you had happened to look through a certain school window recently, you would've seen something that you can see through hundreds of school windows on any given day of the week, all around the world. A schoolgirl, nervously waiting outside the headmistress's office. If you hadn't read this book you might've felt a little bit sorry for the girl, because everyone knows how long the wait outside a headmistress's door can

be. Then you probably would've thought nothing more about it.

But you have read this book, haven't you?

And if someone were to tell you that this particular school was none other than Mossy Blossom Academy for Young Fairies, you would probably guess that this was Elly and that she was feeling very, very uncertain about her future.

The chair that Elly was sitting on while she waited was known as the Chiding-Chair. It had a particularly unpleasant habit of telling anyone who walked by the crimes of the person sitting on it, in a very loud, disapproving voice. Often sitting on the Chiding-Chair was a worse punishment than actually seeing Madame Silverwings. Today the chair was saying, 'Elly dyed her entire class blue!' to anyone who would listen.

Usually this would've made Elly squirm with embarrassment, but today she barely noticed. Her head was buzzing with thoughts. *One day I'm going to start my own fairy school. Everyone will ride skateboards and there'll be no wands.*

She sighed. It was a nice dream but it'd be a long time before it could come true. And it didn't change the fact that she was about to get into a whole lot of trouble. She had dyed a teacher ... *again.* Of course, technically, Madame Silverwings had said she wasn't allowed to dye any more teachers *purple* and Mrs Clovercloud was actually *blue.* And a very attractive shade of blue, at that. But Elly had a feeling that this wouldn't make that much difference to the Head Fairy.

What was she going to tell her parents? Getting expelled had seemed like such a good idea – until it looked like it might actually happen. Maybe she just wouldn't tell them. Maybe she could just pretend she was going to school every day until she figured out what to do.

But when Madame Silverwings finally opened the door Elly realised that this wouldn't work. Her mum and dad were already in Madame Silverwings' office, waiting. Elly gulped and then hurriedly tried to explain the situation. 'It was an accident, Madame Silverwings,' she said. 'My wand has been playing up and I …'

But Madame Silverwings interrupted her. 'Elly,' she said. 'I have just received some very exciting news.'

Elly was suspicious. What was going on? Madame Silverwings was beaming and her parents were looking at her with the proud faces they usually only wore when Kara made some new kind of burping sound. It made Elly nervous.

Madame Silverwings handed her a piece of paper. 'Read it aloud,' she said.

'Successful application for transfer of student from Mossy Blossom Academy to South Street School,' read Elly.

Great. Some lucky student was going to do an exchange at a human school. And to make it worse, it was to Jess's school. Maybe reading the letter out was part of her punishment.

'Isn't it exciting, Elly?' said Elly's mum, smiling. 'It's a great honour, you know.' Elly thought everyone was being very weird.

'I guess it's exciting for whoever it is who's going,' she said, 'but I'd be more excited if it was me.'

Madame Silverwings laughed.

'It *is* you who's going!' she said. 'Why else would I tell you? I sent in an application for exchange on your behalf.'

Elly stared at the Head Fairy in astonishment. 'But I ... but you ...' she stuttered. Madame Silverwings had said that only top students got to go on these exchanges. No-one could possibly consider Elly a top student.

'Your behaviour has vastly improved recently,' explained Madame Silverwings. 'Everyone has commented on it. So it was decided that your, er, *unusual* skills would make you the perfect candidate for an exchange.'

'We always knew your brilliance would shine through eventually,' said Elly's father fondly. 'That's always been clear.'

But only one thing was clear to Elly: there was no way Madame Silverwings knew that she had dyed Mrs Clovercloud blue. If she did, she wouldn't be sending her on a school exchange.

Elly looked around at the adults. They all looked so delighted that suddenly Elly felt bad. She was not a brilliant student and there was no way she deserved the honour

of going on exchange. Elly decided she had to tell them the truth. 'Madame Silverwings,' she said sadly, 'there's something you need to know. This morning I –'

But before she could finish there was a loud noise outside and Gabi Cruddleperry rushed past the window, followed by a trail of squealing piglets, yapping puppies, and clacking scissors.

'Go away!' Gabi shrieked, swatting at them with her hands. But the wand-trails paid absolutely no attention.

'What extraordinary behaviour!' said Madame Silverwings disapprovingly.

'She's got a new wand,' explained Elly, trying not to laugh. She wondered if Gabi was going to get in trouble.

But Madame Silverwings seemed to have

other things on her mind. 'Congratulations, Elly,' she said, leading the Knottleweed-Eversprightlys to the door. 'I do hope you'll drop by one day.' She opened the door.

'But Madame Silverwings,' protested Elly, 'there's something important I have to tell you. Something that changes everything.'

But it was as if Madame Silverwings didn't want to hear what Elly had to say. 'Oh, it can't be that important, surely!' she said, ushering the family out of the room. 'It's been a pleasure knowing you, Elly. You are a very original fairy.'

Then she shook Elly's hand vigorously and closed the door – but just before she did, Elly glimpsed something lying on Madame Silverwings' desk. A silver rod, a star and some shards of plastic, all surrounded by a pool of blue ink. Elly was astonished. Was it possible that Madame Silverwings knew about what had happened in Mrs Clovercloud's class after all? She tried to take another look, but before she could, the Head Fairy firmly closed the door.

'Well, you've clearly made a very strong impression on her,' said Mrs Knottleweed-Eversprightly proudly.

But Elly wasn't listening. She could've sworn she heard Madame Silverwings say, as if to herself, 'A *very* original fairy indeed – but please don't come back!'